04 July 2008

- This is for our nation's bravest warriors . . . our generations, our children —

God Bless!
Gary Stenson
(LIEUTENANT GARY)

To order additional copies of this book, contact LT Gary at
www.neverfarapart.com or 619-540-0332

LT Gary is a Naval Officer and has been a Navy SEAL for over 20 years. As a SEAL, he was away often, as are all military parents. While deployed to Afghanistan following events of 11 September, 2001, he wrote down the words to a lullaby he'd typically sing to his son when he put him to bed at night. LT Gary never imagined he'd return from that deployment to an empty home. The last page in the book is the song he wrote for his son entitled "SS Rock-a-Bye". LT Gary's story (as well as the song he wrote for his son) has been the focus of websites nationwide. Additionally, FOX News ran the story with the song. He has testified before the California State Senate regarding his case along side of a female Army Officer who lost her children as a result of her service to country. Lieutenant Gary dedicates this book to his son Sean, to his parents, and to his wife. He dedicates this book to those thousands of men and women serving in our armed forces worldwide who have lost their parental rights as a result of their service to country, and as a result of the absence of federal laws in place to ensure U.S. jurisdiction over their children while they are away preserving "our way of life" for families back home. LT Gary's book, "Never Far Apart" is about separation, and the undying love a parent feels for a child even when they are unable to physically be there with the child to show them that love on a daily basis.

Sweet child of mine I miss you,
and I know you miss me too.
And the time seems like forever
when I can't be there with you.

But you're here with me each second,
and each minute of each day.
You're here with me each and every night
when I bow my head to pray.

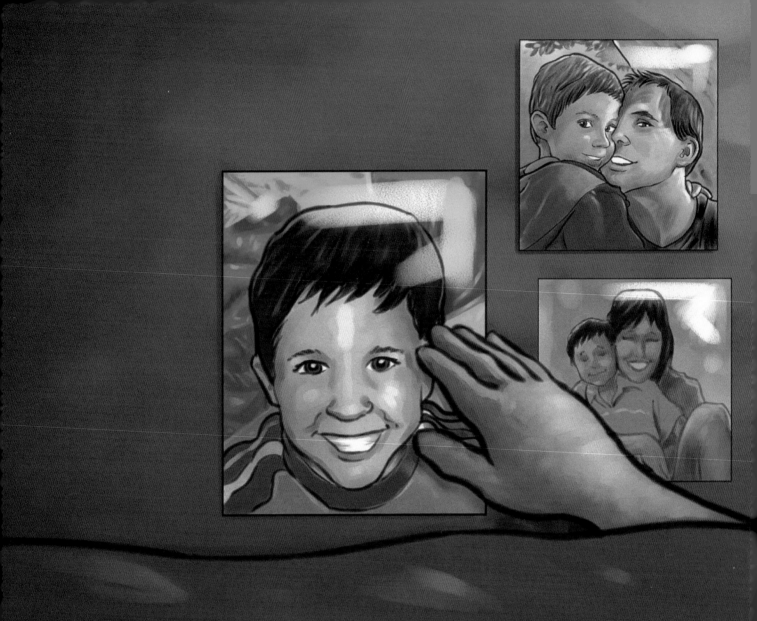

You're here with me each morning.
You are my rising sun.
You're here with me each evening saying,
"another day is done."

Sweet child of mine I know you're sad,
and heavy is your heart.
When it seems time passes slowly,
know we're never far apart.

There's one connected ocean,
and there's one connected sky.
Each mountain rolls into another,
under God's protective eyes.
He's always there to watch me,
and return me back to you.
He's always there to listen,
and He does some talking too.
He whispers to me soft, sweet songs,
of you my child so brave and strong.
And sometimes Daddy sheds a tear,
when He sings lullabies of you inside my ears.

Sweet child of mine I love you,
with each beat inside my chest.
You're the air that gives me life,
so I can take another step.

I close my eyes and remember
what it feels like cheek to cheek.
I see your smile, and it's like
I'm standing on a mountain's peak.

I feel your arms as they wrap themselves
around my neck so tight.
They are the bridge connecting me
to you my little knight.

Sweet child of mine I'm there with you,
just close your eyes and see.
I'm in your heart and whispering that
you ARE the world to me.

I remember the moment you were born,
and I took you in my arms.
Your eyes began to open saying,
"just keep me safe from harm."
That's what I've done and will always do,
even when I'm not there next to you.
I'll protect you and love you no matter what,
and I'll be back with you in a lickety cut!

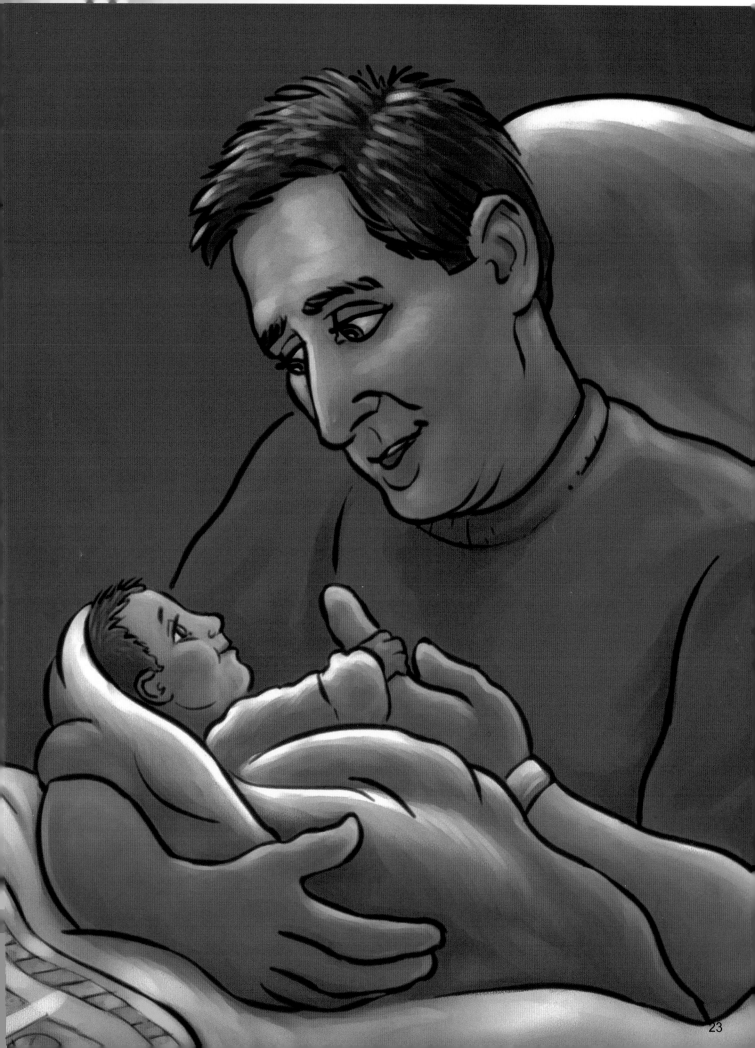

"SS Rock-a-Bye"

17 May 2002

C 2006

By: Lieutenant Gary

Verse one:

Rock a bye SS ROCK Rock a Bye you sang to me each eve . . .

And you gave me rolling rock a byes of dreams I've yet to dream.

Each night I'd pray that when I'd awake . . .

You'd have safely ROCK'd me home ...

to the greatest gift, the Lord hath given me; my little

child named Sean. (YOUR CHILD'S NAME IN HERE)

CHORUS:

Daddy's ship is back in town and this time it's for good.

Please understand . . .

Please know that I'd have been there if I could.

But things just aren't so simple on a haze grey lullaby . . .

this ship I'll call the ever lonely - SS ROCK A BYE.

VERSE TWO:

I can count the shorelines that I've past like others count their sheep.

I saw shadows dancing in the night . . . while you rock'd me down to sleep.

But last night I knew that when I'd awake,

I'd hold you in my arms . . .

To personally protect you and . . .

to keep you safe from harm.

REPEAT CHORUS

Daddy's ship is back in town and this time its for good.

Please understand

Please know that I'd have been there if I could.

But things just aren't so simple on a haze grey lullaby . . .

this ship I'll call the ever lonely

. . . SS ROCK A BYE

this ship we'll call the ever lonely

. . . SS ROCK A BYE